THIS CANDLEWICK BOOK BELONGS TO:

_____

_____

_____

_____

For Alexia

First U.S. paperback edition 1995

Library of Congress Cataloging-in-Publication Data

Miller, Virginia.
Go to bed! / Virginia Miller.—1st U.S. ed.

Summary: A little bear resists going to bed as long as he can.
ISBN 1-56402-244-7 (hardcover)—ISBN 1-56402-509-8 (paperback)
[1. Bears—Fiction.   2. Bedtime—Fiction.]   I. Title.
PZ7.M6373Go   1993
[E]—dc20   92-54958

2 4 6 8 10 9 7 5 3 1

Printed in Hong Kong

The pictures in this book were done in soft pencil and pantone markers.

Candlewick Press, 2067 Massachusetts Avenue, Cambridge, Massachusetts 02140

GO TO BED!

Virginia Miller

CANDLEWICK PRESS
CAMBRIDGE, MASSACHUSETTS

It was time for Bartholomew to go to bed.
"Ba, time for bed," George said.
"Nah!" said Bartholomew.

George said, "Brush your teeth and go to bed."

"Nah!" said Bartholomew.

"Have you brushed your teeth yet, Ba?"

"Nah!" said Bartholomew, beginning to cry.

"Come on, Ba, into bed!" George said.
"Nah!" said Bartholomew.

"Nah, nah, nah, nah,

NAH!" said Bartholomew.

George said in a big voice.

Bartholomew got into bed. He giggled

and wriggled,

he hid

and tiggled,

he cuddled

and huggled,

he snuggled

and sighed.

"Good night, Bartholomew," said George.

"Nah," said Bartholomew softly.

He gave a big yawn, closed his eyes,

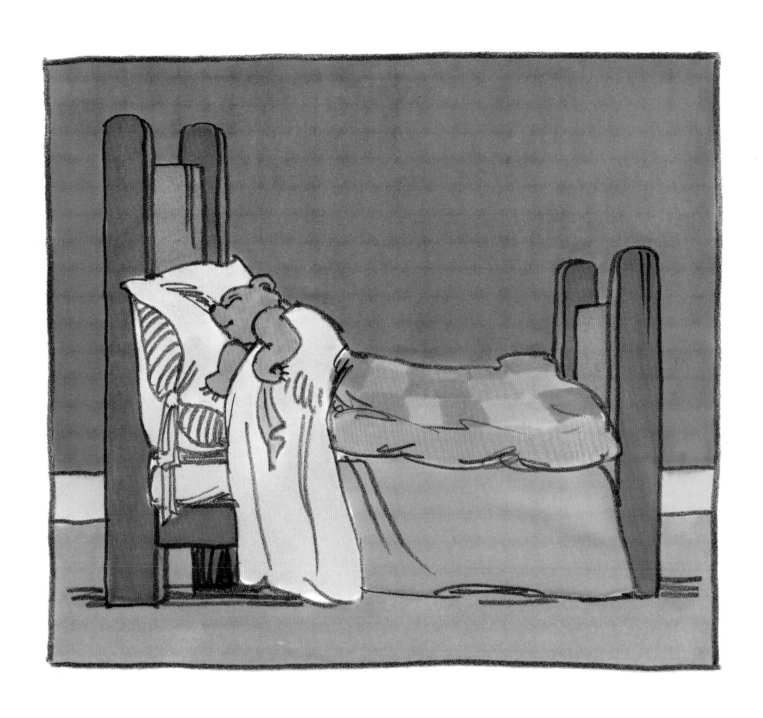

and went to sleep.

VIRGINIA MILLER wrote *Go to Bed!* as a follow-up to her earlier
Bartholomew and George stories, *On Your Potty!* and *Eat Your Dinner!*
She says, "These books are intended to help make light of common parent-child
conflicts because if they make you smile, things don't seem so bad."